JACK FROST

First published 2009 by Macmillan Children's Books
This edition published 2011 by Macmillan Children's Books
a division of Macmillan Publishers Limited
20 New Wharf Road, London N1 9RR
Basingstoke and Oxford
Associated companies throughout the world
www.panmacmillan.com

ISBN: 978-1-4472-0268-4

3 5 7 9 8 6 4 2

A CIP catalogue record for this book is available
from the British Library.

Printed in China

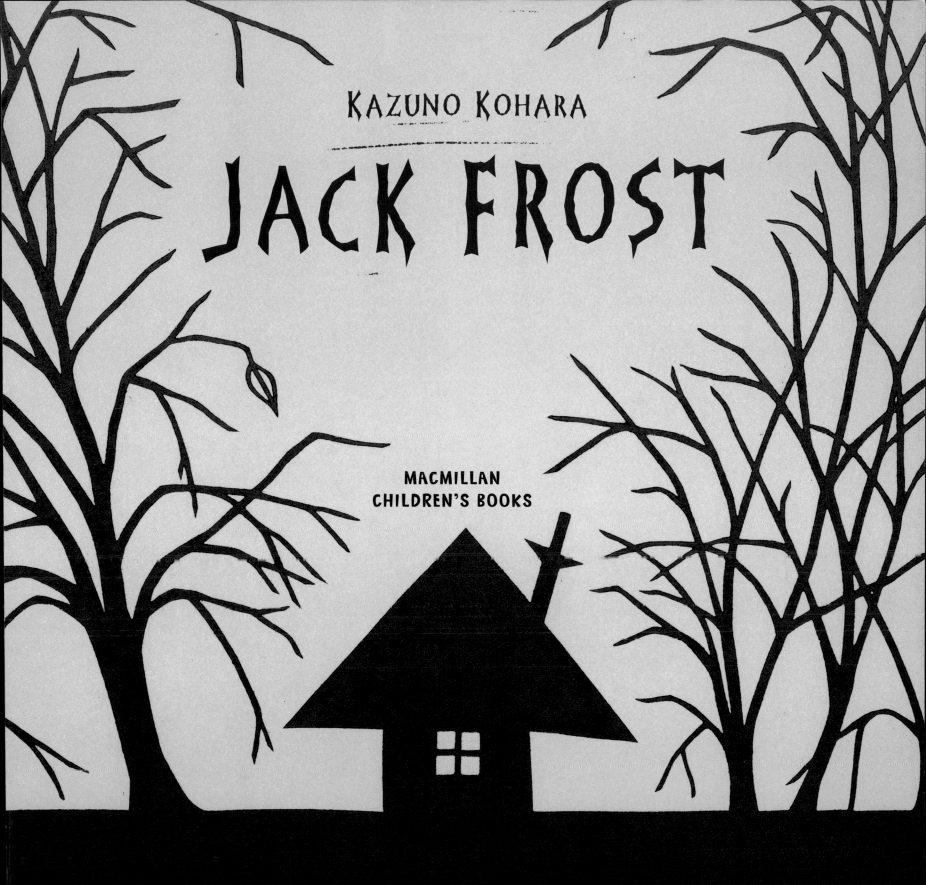

KAZUNO KOHARA

JACK FROST

MACMILLAN
CHILDREN'S BOOKS

Once there was a boy who lived in a house in the woods. It was winter, and all his friends were hibernating.

"I hate winter," he sighed.

But then, one cold morning . . .

. . . strange patterns
appeared on the window!

The boy ran outside, and saw a white figure
covering his house with frost and ice.

"Who are you?" asked the boy.
"I'm Jack Frost!" replied the figure,

and he ran into the woods.
"Wait!" cried the boy, and chased after him.

"You can't catch me!"
laughed Jack Frost.
"You can't jump over
the pond!"

But the boy had ice skates.

"You can't catch me!"
cried Jack Frost.
"You can't jump over
the hill!"

But the boy had a sledge.

Jack Frost threw a snowball at the boy.
He threw one back!

"Will you stay and play with me?" asked the boy.
"Yes," smiled Jack Frost, "but never mention
anything warm in front of me . . .

that would break the spell
and force me to leave. But now
there are so many things we can do."

"I know," said the boy. "Let's build snowmen!"

They built three, so that they
wouldn't feel lonely.

All winter, the boy was careful not to mention anything warm.

Until one day . . .

They were playing
hide-and-seek in the woods when
the boy found something.

It was a snowdrop.

"Look, Jack Frost!" said the boy.

"It's almost spring . . ."

But Jack Frost was
no longer there.
The spell was broken.

But in the wind that went
through the woods,
the boy was sure he heard
a whisper . . .

"See you next winter!"